The Secret Garden

Treasury of Illustrated Classics™

The Secret Garden

by
Frances Hodgson Burnett

Adapted by
Devra Newberger Speregen

Illustrated by
Richard Lauter

Modern Publishing
A Division of Unisystems, Inc.
New York, New York 10022

Series UPC: 39360

Cover art by Richard Lauter

Contents

PART THREE

PART FOUR

Part

1

Chapter

A New Life

$\mathbb{M}$ary Lennox gazed through the train window at the dark gray sky. It was raining hard, and the heavy raindrops pelted loudly against the window as the train rumbled across the English countryside.

Staring out at the rainstorm, Mary frowned. She didn't particularly like sitting in a damp, musty train. Nor did she like having to travel with Mrs. Medlock, the unpleasant old woman sent to take care of Mary on the journey to

Misselthwaite Manor. More than anything, however, Mary didn't like having
to come here to England to live with her
strange uncle, a man she had never
even met.

Mary watched as the train cruised
past tiny villages and trees. Everything
looked so foreign and strange. It wasn't
anything like India, where Mary had lived
her whole life.

The sky, so gray and dark, seemed to
fit Mary's unpleasant mood. Mary sighed
loudly and sat back in her seat. She
turned away from the window and stole a
glance at Mrs. Medlock, who was lost in
her own thoughts. Mary could tell by
Mrs. Medlock's sour expression that she
was not happy about having to take care
of her. Nobody had ever wanted to take
care of Mary.

Though Mary grew up in a grand
palace in India with hundreds of servants,
she had been alone most of the time. In
fact, Mary rarely ever saw her parents.
Her father worked for the English govern-

ment and was too concerned with his work to pay any attention to her. Mary's mother was young and beautiful and cared more about attending parties than spending time with her daughter.

Mary was raised by a Nanny, or Ayah, as she called her. Her Ayah tended to her every day, cooking for her, cleaning up after her, even dressing her. Now nine years old, Mary didn't even know how to dress herself.

Mary grew to have a terrible temper. She ordered her servants and her Ayah around so much that nobody could stand to be near her. It wasn't long before Mary grew from a spoiled baby to a spoiled, ill-tempered child who almost never smiled. Because of this, Mary didn't have any friends at all.

One winter morning, her Ayah did not come to wake and dress her. Later, Mary learned that her Ayah had passed away from a terrible sickness. Within days that sickness spread across India, killing many people, including Mary's parents. Left all alone in the world, she would have to be sent to live with her uncle, Lord Archibald Craven, at Misselthwaite Manor in England.

Mary traveled by boat to England, where Mrs. Medlock met her at the train station. Mrs. Medlock looked very disappointed when she saw the young girl.

"Such a plain, frail child!" she remarked to a conductor, loud enough for Mary to hear. "We had heard her mother was a beauty. She didn't hand much of it down, did she?"

Mary didn't care too much for Mrs. Medlock, either. She had a stern, sour face and wore dark clothes. Mary hoped everyone else in England wasn't as unpleasant.

The train slowed to a stop, and Mrs. Medlock turned to Mary and spoke, interrupting Mary's thoughts. "I suppose I may as well tell you something about where you are going," she said flatly. "Do you know anything about your uncle?"

Mary shook her head. "No," she replied.

"Your father and mother never spoke of him?" Mrs. Medlock asked in surprise.

"No," Mary said again. Her parents had never talked to her about anything in particular.

Mrs. Medlock seemed shocked. "Well, I suppose you might as well be told something, so you'll be prepared," she said. "You are going to a very strange place."

Mary said nothing and stared out the train window as she listened to Mrs.

Medlock describe Misselthwaite Manor. The Manor was very old, almost six hundred years old. It was huge, too, like a castle. It had nearly a hundred rooms. But the strangest thing about the Manor, Mary thought, was something called "the moor." Mrs. Medlock said it surrounded Misselthwaite Manor for miles and miles.

"Most of the rooms in the house are shut and locked up," Mrs. Medlock told Mary. "You'll have your space to play

about and look after yourself, but you'll be warned which rooms to stay away from. There are many gardens, too. Some of them are kept up rather nicely. Outside, you may go wherever you please, but in the house, you mustn't ever go poking about."

"I won't ...," Mary started.

"As for your uncle," Mrs. Medlock continued, "he's not going to trouble himself with you, that's for sure. He never troubles himself with anyone. In fact, he's out of the country now and will probably be gone for quite a while."

Mrs. Medlock waited for Mary to ask more about her uncle, but Mary just continued to stare out the window.

"He's got a crooked back," Mrs. Medlock went on, "and until he married your aunt, he was a sour young man with a lot of money. They were very happy together. Then, when she died ..."

Mary spun around in her seat and looked at Mrs. Medlock. "She died?" Mary asked.

"Yes," Mrs. Medlock replied. "And it made Lord Craven stranger than ever. He didn't want to see anybody, and he still doesn't. Most of the time he just goes away. When he's at the Manor, he shuts himself up in the west wing and doesn't let anybody see him."

Mary turned back to the train window and watched the rain again. She wished she were back in India. At least in India there had been no strange uncles or bitter, old caretakers.

Mary watched the rain until her eyes grew heavy. She fell asleep to the patter of the raindrops against the pane.

Chapter

2

Hearing a Secret

W hen Mary arrived at Misselthwaite Manor, she was shown to a large, gloomy room with portraits of hunters and dogs hanging on the walls. Outside her window she could see a great stretch of land that seemed to have no trees on it and looked rather like an endless purple sea.

"That is the moor," explained a young housemaid. "Do you like it?"

Mary stared at the housemaid, then turned back to the window. "No," she replied coldly. "I hate it."

Martha, the housemaid, continued tidying up Mary's room and unpacking her things. If she noticed Mary's rude tone, she didn't show it. She went on cheerfully polishing the furniture and tending to the fire in the fireplace.

"Well, I just love it!" she told Mary. "It's covered with sweet-smelling things and grows lovely in the spring. I wouldn't live away from the moor for anything! The name's Martha," she added.

Mary scoffed at her strange new servant. Back in India, servants weren't any-

thing like Martha. They did not talk to their masters as if they were their equals. They bowed and called them "master" and "sir."

"Are you going to dress me?" Mary asked Martha, not bothering to introduce herself.

Martha seemed surprised. "Can't you dress yourself?" she asked.

"No," Mary answered impatiently. "I never have in my whole life. My Ayah dressed me, of course."

Martha threw up her hands. "Well!" she said with a laugh. "It's time you learned!"

Mary grew angry at once. "I will not be laughed at by a servant!" she cried.

Martha stared at Mary in disbelief. The poor girl, she thought. No father, no mother, no brothers or sisters. She must be so lonely. Martha didn't know what it was to be lonely. She had twelve brothers and sisters. She decided to ignore Mary's rude behavior. Hopefully, Martha thought, she would become friendlier in time.

Martha poured Mary some tea and began to talk about her brothers and sisters, especially about her younger brother Dickon. Although Mary was in a foul mood, and pretended not to listen, she couldn't help but smile at Martha's funny stories.

Martha said that Dickon was one of the friendliest, happiest people she knew. He knew how to make friends with the animals on the moor. Dickon had even befriended a wild pony, and now the pony followed Dickon around wherever he went.

Mary thought she might like to see that. She'd never seen a boy who made friends with animals. Soon, she was listening very closely to Martha and even laughing out loud at times.

When Martha was finished cleaning Mary's room, she told Mary to go off to play.

"But who will go with me?" Mary asked.

"You'll go by yourself," Martha answered. "You'll have to learn how to play by yourself, like Dickon. That's how he made friends with that pony. He's even made friends with the sheep and birds on the moor, that Dickon!"

All the talk about Dickon made Mary more curious than ever to meet him.

"You'll meet him someday," Martha assured her. She helped Mary put on her coat and hat and showed her to the door.

"If you go around that way," Martha said, "you'll find the gardens. There are

lots of flowers in the summertime, but it's pretty barren now." She hesitated for a second. "One of the gardens is locked up, so you won't be able to see it. No one has seen it in ten years."

"Why?" Mary asked.

Martha bit her lip, wondering if she should tell Mary about the locked garden. She lowered her voice and explained that Lord Craven had the garden closed immediately after his wife died.

Mary's eyes widened.

"He's locked the door and buried the key in the ground," Martha added. Then she realized she'd said more than enough. She quickly ushered Mary out the door.

Chapter

3

Ben and the Robin

Walking along the paths by the gardens, Mary couldn't help but think about the locked-up garden. How could such a thing be closed? Couldn't you always walk in a garden? She kept walking, wondering what the garden looked like.

Suddenly she came upon an old man with a spade, who was bent over the earth planting seeds. He was startled to see Mary, but he tipped his hat politely and went back to planting.

"What is this place?" Mary asked,

again not bothering to introduce herself. She was looking at all the plain bushes around her, with a displeased expression on her face.

"One of the kitchen gardens," he answered. "The vegetables for the Manor are all grown here."

"And that?" she demanded, pointing to a green door.

"Another kitchen garden," the old man replied shortly, displeased by Mary's intrusion.

"Can I go in there?" Mary asked.

"If you want to," he answered with a shrug. "But there's nothing to see."

Mary didn't respond. Instead, she walked down the path and through the door. The man had been right. The garden had only winter vegetables.

Over on the other side of the garden, Mary saw another green door.

"Maybe that's the door to the mysterious garden," she thought. Without hesitating, she ran to the door, hoping that it wouldn't open and that it was the mysterious locked door. But it opened quite easily, and she found herself in an orchard with fruit trees.

Mary looked around anxiously, but there were no more green doors. What she did see, however, was a high wall covered

with ivy. It was a long wall, too, and it seemed to go on and on. Over the top of it, Mary saw treetops and birds sitting on a high branch and staring down at her.

A robin burst into song, as if he were singing to Mary. Although Mary was feeling sad and lonely, she managed to smile and continued to listen to him sing until he flew away over the wall. She wondered if the mysterious, locked-up garden was on the other side of the wall and if the robin lived there.

On her way back to the Manor, Mary thought and thought about the garden. She was so curious, she felt she might burst! She dreamed of what it might look like, and she wondered why her uncle had locked it and buried the key. Would she ever meet her uncle? If she did, would she be brave enough to ask him about the garden?

While thinking of all these thoughts, she again came upon the old man, who was still digging and planting in the vegetable garden. Mary stood beside him for a while, then finally spoke.

"I have been in the other gardens," she announced. "And in the orchard."

The man kept digging and didn't respond. Like Martha, he just didn't like Mary's rudeness.

"But there was no door into this other garden," Mary said.

The man put down his spade and cast a stern look at Mary. "What garden?" he asked.

"The one on the other side of the high wall," Mary replied. "I know there is a garden there. I saw the tops of trees, and a bird with a red breast flew in there."

She waited to hear what the old man would say, but he didn't say anything. Instead, he turned toward the orchard and whistled. Suddenly, there was a whooshing noise above her head, and Mary gazed up. The robin! He had answered the old man's call!

Mary watched as the robin flew about, circling the old man. He certainly

was a charming, friendly little bird.

The gardener watched the bird for a while, then turned to Mary.

"Are you Lord Craven's niece from India?" he asked.

Mary nodded. "Who are you?" she asked.

"Ben Weatherstaff," the gardener answered. Then he pointed to the robin. "And this here's my only friend."

Mary gazed admiringly at the robin, which was pecking at the earth, looking for food.

"I have no friends at all," she said flatly. "I never have had any. My Ayah didn't even like me, and I never played with anyone."

Ben Weatherstaff stared at Mary. She was obviously a very lonely little girl. Seeing her thin, pale face and her sad eyes, he felt sorry for her.

Suddenly, the robin burst into song and landed on a branch right beside Mary.

"Looks like you have a friend now!" Ben Weatherstaff chuckled.

Mary reached out for the robin, but he flew up and away, over the gardens and over the orchard wall.

"Does he live in that garden?" Mary asked. "The one over the high wall?"

"Probably," Ben Weatherstaff answered. "Among the rose trees."

"Oh! There are rose trees there?" Mary asked excitedly. "Have you been there?"

Ben Weatherstaff picked up his spade

and began to dig again. "A long time ago," he mumbled.

"I should like to see the garden!" Mary announced suddenly. "Where is the door? There must be a door somewhere!"

Ben Weatherstaff shifted uncomfortably. "Listen, I must get back to work. You shouldn't go poking around here! Now go on! I have no more time for you!" With that, he flung his spade over his shoulder and walked off, without even saying good-bye.

Chapter

Lady Craven

In the days that followed, Mary began to get used to her new life. She woke every morning and spent time with Martha, who told stories about her brothers and sisters while she polished the furniture and arranged breakfast. Mary especially loved hearing about Dickon.

After breakfast Mary would go outside alone to play. She would explore the enormous gardens, each day finding a new path and noticing a new flower or bird.

"The fresh air suits you!" Martha

exclaimed one afternoon, after Mary had been there a week.

Mary had to agree. She had color in her face and felt healthier than ever. She looked very different from the sad, disagreeable young thing Mrs. Medlock had met at the train station. Even her hair shined.

Mary's uncle had still not returned from his travel abroad. Mary wondered if he ever would. She also wondered what he would think of her. Perhaps, she thought, he knew he would not like her. Perhaps her father and mother had told him how unfriendly she was. Maybe that was why he stayed away. He probably didn't want to meet her.

Meanwhile, Mary kept herself busy looking for the mysterious garden. She still could not find the door, though she walked along the high wall day after day. Ben Weatherstaff had said there was no door. But, she thought, there had to be a door! Her uncle had buried the key!

The mystery gave her so much to think about and made her so curious, that finding the door seemed to be all she cared about. Back in India, Mary hadn't cared about anything.

Every evening, while Martha prepared her supper, Mary listened to more of Martha's stories about Dickon and his animal friends of the moor. One evening,

Mary got up the courage to ask Martha about the garden.

"Why did my uncle hate the garden?" she asked.

"It was Lady Craven's garden," Martha explained. "She made it when they were married. They used to go into that garden together and sit for hours in a big tree that had a limb shaped like a seat. They loved that garden so! But one day, Lady Craven fell from the tree when the limb broke off. She was hurt so badly, she died the next day. That's why Lord Craven hates the garden so. That's why he's locked it up and doesn't let anyone go in."

Mary stared at the fire in her fireplace. What a sad story, she thought. Her uncle must have been crushed when his wife died. The wind howled loudly outside her window, sending a shiver up Mary's back.

Suddenly, she heard a strange sound above the howl of the wind. It sounded like the wind, but it wasn't. Mary gasped.

It was the sound of someone crying!

"Do you hear anyone crying?" she asked Martha.

Martha looked away nervously. "No," she answered abruptly. "It's the wind you hear."

"But listen," Mary insisted. "It's coming from inside the house, somewhere down one of those long corridors!"

At that very moment, a gust of wind blew open a door somewhere on the other side of the huge house. The crying sounded even louder.

"There!" Mary said. "I told you! It is someone crying. It sounds like . . . a child!"

Martha jumped up and shut the door to Mary's room. "It was the wind," she said sternly. "And if it wasn't, it was probably Betty Butterworth, the kitchen maid. She's had a toothache all day!"

There was something about the expression on Martha's face that gave her away. Mary knew immediately that she was hiding something.

Chapter

Finding the Key

After a few days of constant rain, it was finally nice enough to play outdoors again. Mary finished breakfast and rushed out of the house, and was met by a bright blue sky.

The first thing she did was to run ten times around the flower garden behind the Manor. Then she ran to the kitchen gardens. She'd been cooped up for so long, she had lots of energy.

Running along, she finally came to a stop when she found Ben Weatherstaff.

"Springtime's comin'!" he said. "Can't you smell it?"

Mary sniffed deeply. Yes! She could smell the spring coming! She smiled. The thought of spring excited her. It was funny, she thought. She couldn't remember being excited about anything in her whole life.

Mary stood with her eyes closed and her face toward the sun. Suddenly she heard the soft rustling of tree branches and the sound of a bird chirping. She knew it was her robin!

Mary opened her eyes and saw him hopping on a nearby branch. She clapped her hands together joyfully. The robin flew so close to Mary, it made her tremble with excitement.

"He remembers me!" Mary cried happily. She thought to herself, right at that very second, that perhaps England was not so bad. It was here in England, at Misselthwaite Manor, that she had found people to like. Never before had Mary liked anybody, but now she liked Martha and Martha's brother Dickon, though she had never met him. And she most definitely liked this robin!

With a chirp, the robin set out, flying toward the orchard. Mary ran after him. She watched as the robin landed on a branch and sang, bobbing his head from side to side. Mary thought he looked very beautiful, with his satiny waistcoat and his chest puffed so proudly as he chirped. Then, all at once, the robin took off again, this time landing on another branch along the wall.

"He wants me to follow him!" Mary realized with excitement. She skipped after the robin, chirping back to him, pretending to speak to him in his language. "I'm talking to creatures, just like Dickon does!" Mary thought with a smile.

Mary followed the robin from tree to tree until he landed on the ground beside a tiny pile of freshly dug earth. Next to the pile was a hole in the ground.

Mary looked in. Something was half-buried in the soil. It was a piece of metal. She reached out to pick it up and gasped in shock. It was a key, an old key that looked as though it had been buried a long time!

Mary could scarcely breathe. She lifted the key from the dirt and studied it closely.

"Could it be?" she asked the robin. "Could this key I'm holding be the key to the secret garden?"

Part

2

Chapter

6

The Robin Helps Again

Mary lay awake in her bed for nearly half the night. Every once in a while, she would reach under her pillow and touch the key. She wondered if it was indeed the key that opened the door to the secret garden. If it was, all she had to do now was find the door.

When Mary finally fell asleep, she dreamed of finding the door and unlocking it with her key. She dreamed of playing in the garden with Martha and Dickon. She had heard so many wonderful stories about Dickon, she felt as if she'd known him forever.

Mary awoke the next morning as Martha was bringing in her breakfast tray. On the tray was Mary's usual bowl of porridge and her usual cup of tea and a biscuit. There was also something else. There was a small bag next to her tea cup.

"Go ahead, open it!" Martha urged. "It's a present!"

"A present!" Mary exclaimed.

Mary was very surprised that Martha had bought her a present. She knew that Martha was poor and lived in a small cottage with all those brothers and sisters. It was a generous gift.

"Open it!" Martha cried again.

Mary reached into the bag and pulled out a strong, slender rope with a red and blue striped handle at each end. She looked at it curiously. Mary had never seen a jump rope before.

"It's for skipping," Martha told her.

Martha showed Mary how to use the jump rope, and soon Mary was skipping

all through the Manor. She couldn't wait to get outside.

"Thank you, Martha," Mary said uncomfortably. She had never thanked anyone in her life. She wasn't used to saying the words.

"Don't mention it," Martha told her. She smiled and handed Mary her coat and hat, ushering her outdoors to skip.

It wasn't long before Mary was skipping as if she'd always known how. Pretty soon she was skipping through the gardens, making up songs, and singing as she skipped. She skipped until she was out of breath and had to stop.

Mary rested along the high wall of the locked-up garden. She gazed along the wall and thought about how it seemed to go on forever. Picking up her rope, she decided that she would skip along the wall as far as possible. Maybe she could skip the whole length of it.

Mary set off skipping, and moments later something red appeared in the sky. It was her robin!

"You showed me where the key was yesterday," Mary called to him. "Can you show me where the door is today?"

She thought it was a silly question to ask a robin, which most likely didn't understand her. To her surprise, however,

the robin chirped a loud message back to her and took off from his branch.

Mary followed him as quickly as she could, sometimes forgetting to skip. She was a little out of breath when the robin stopped and settled on top of the high wall. He was staring down at her.

Mary looked closely at the wall beneath the robin. It was covered with thick ivy that had never been trimmed and had grown wild. It was so thick that even a strong gust of wind could not rustle it.

Reaching down to pick up her jump rope, she saw a flicker of light beneath the ivy. In a flash, Mary ran to the wall and began to push away the thick ivy branches that grew there. Something other than stone was underneath. Mary pushed more ivy away, then gasped in amazement at what she saw.

A wooden door!

Mary's heart thumped wildly, and her hands shook with excitement. Quickly, she cleared away as much ivy as possible.

The robin sang as he watched Mary uncover the old wooden door. He then chirped with delight when Mary found the door's keyhole.

Mary dug into her dress pocket and pulled out the key that she'd found the day before. Taking a deep breath, she put the key into the keyhole. It fit! Using all her strength, she turned the key.

She couldn't believe what was happening. With a quick glance down the path, making sure no one was coming, Mary took another deep breath and leaned her small body against the big, heavy door. She pushed with all her might. Slowly, very slowly, the door opened.

When it was open just enough for her to fit through, Mary slipped through the door and closed it behind her. Resting against it, she gazed around in amazement. Her heart thumped even faster than before.

She was standing inside the secret garden!

Chapter

Entering the Garden

"How still it is," Mary whispered to herself as she walked through the garden. Everywhere she looked, she saw rose trees and ivy so thick it was matted together. The ground was covered with winter's brown grass and clumps of rose bushes that no longer seemed alive. There were other trees and plants in the garden, too, which Mary imagined had once been quite beautiful.

"I am the first person in this garden in ten years!" she exclaimed softly.

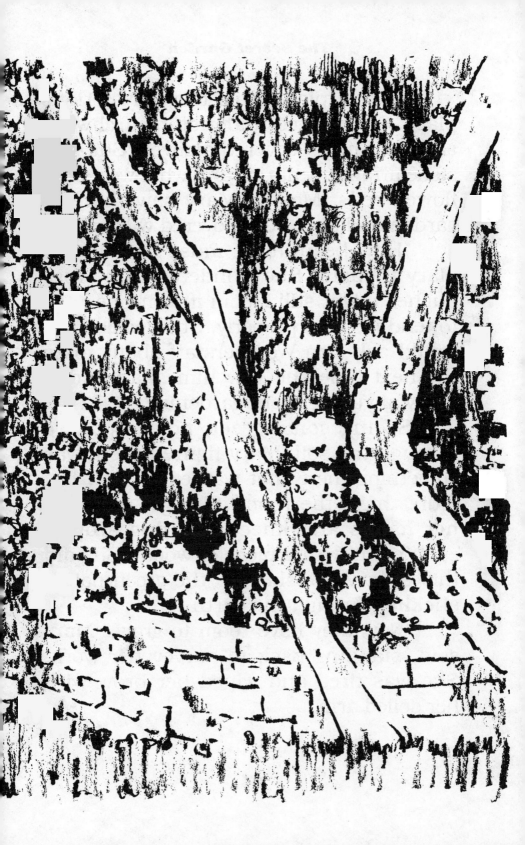

Mary explored this new, mysterious place. She walked under stone archways and past moss-covered alcoves. She saw stone arrangements around what were once flower beds. Mostly, Mary saw that the garden had once been covered with roses.

"How beautiful it must have been!" Mary thought. She wondered if the rose bushes might still bloom if someone were to tend to them properly. She decided she would ask Ben Weatherstaff about roses the next time she saw him. Mary didn't know anything about gardening.

Seeing some green points poking through the soil, Mary figured there was something there that wanted to grow but didn't have the room. She got down on her hands and knees and dug around each point with a piece of wood. She did this everywhere she saw the green points sticking through the earth.

"Now they have room to grow," Mary said, standing back to survey her work. She was tired and wiped her brow with her soiled arm.

"I'm going to do more. I'll do all I can. I'll come back every day and work more."

Mary went from place to place, digging and weeding. She enjoyed herself so much that she lost track of time. Before she knew it, it was almost time for lunch.

Back at the Manor, Mary ate two helpings of meat. Martha was pleased that Mary had a healthy appetite. When Mary had first come to Misselthwaite Manor, she had been a thin, pale child. Now Mary had rosy cheeks and was full of energy. Martha also noted that Mary had become a whole lot friendlier.

"My, have you changed!" Martha exclaimed.

Mary told Martha she'd been digging all morning. Of course, she didn't tell Martha she'd been in the locked-up garden. That was a secret Mary wasn't ready to share. But she told Martha she'd found a bit of land where she wanted to grow things.

"But I don't know anything about growing things," Mary sulked.

"Dickon does!" Martha said excitedly. "He knows all about growing things. Dickon can make a flower grow out of a brick wall!"

Mary laughed.

"Dickon can get some seeds for you," Martha said. "He'll know what to buy. When he comes to visit, he can help you with your little garden."

Mary couldn't believe what she was hearing.

"Dickon is coming to visit?" she asked in amazement. "Oh, that would be so nice! I would so much like to meet your brother!"

It was then decided that Dickon

would buy seeds for Mary's garden and bring them to her. Mary could hardly wait.

The sun shone down for nearly a week on the secret garden. The Secret Garden was what Mary decided to call it. She liked having a secret. But most of all, she liked the feeling she got when she went into the Secret Garden all by herself. Shut in by its high walls, she felt free to do whatever she pleased. It was like a magical place she had only read about in fairy tales.

During that week, Mary saw Ben Weatherstaff a couple of times and she

managed to ask him some questions about planting. She told him she had a little garden of her own and wanted to plant roses. Ben looked sad for a moment.

"I once knew another young lady who loved roses," he said softly.

"Where is she now?" Mary asked.

"In heaven," Ben said.

Mary had a feeling Ben was talking about her aunt, Lady Craven.

"What happened to the roses?" Mary asked. "Did they die? Do roses die when they are left to themselves?"

"They run wild," Ben explained. "Most will die, but some live."

"How can you tell if they are alive?" Mary asked, hoping that Ben wouldn't become too suspicious from all her questions about roses.

"Wait until the spring," he told her. "Wait until the sun shines on them and the rain falls on them. Then see what happens. If they're alive, they'll blossom."

Chapter

8

Meeting Dickon

One sunny morning, Mary skipped toward the Secret Garden, eager to dig and weed until it was time for lunch. She skipped happily for a while, but stopped short when she heard a peculiar whistling coming from a nearby alcove.

Mary hid behind a tree and quietly peered into the alcove. She saw a boy sitting with his back against a tree, playing a wooden pipe. He was a funny-looking boy, about twelve years old. He had a turned-up nose, and his cheeks were as red as poppies. Mary had never seen such blue eyes on anyone before.

Meanwhile, on the branches of the tree under which the boy sat, a little squirrel was listening. On the ground a few feet away from the boy, there were two rabbits. It appeared to Mary as if the rabbits were listening, too!

"Don't move!" the boy called out softly. "It'll scare them."

Mary stood perfectly still. The boy stopped playing his flute and slowly got up. Mary watched in amazement as the animals went about their business, not scared in the least.

The boy smiled at Mary. "I'm Dickon," he said to her. "And you must be Miss Mary."

Somehow, Mary had known this was Dickon, even before he told her his name. Who else could have been charming squirrels and rabbits?

"I got up slowly, because if you move suddenly, it scares them," Dickon explained. "You have to move gently and speak quietly when animals are about."

Mary could hardly contain her excitement. Dickon was so nice! He spoke to her as if he'd known her for years, as if they had always been friends.

"Did you get the seeds?" Mary asked shyly.

Dickon nodded. "And I've brought

garden tools, too!" he said happily. Dickon showed Mary the different seeds he had. "These are poppy seeds, and these are larkspur. The poppies are the sweetest things you'll ever smell!"

Suddenly, Dickon lifted his chin and gazed up in the sky. His face lit up and his smile was big and bright. "Do you hear that robin?" he asked. "He's calling to you!"

"Is he really?" Mary asked excitedly. It was the red-breasted robin, and he was talking to her! If Dickon said he was, then it had to be true, Mary decided.

"Yes. He's saying, 'Here I am!'" Dickon laughed.

"Do you understand everything birds say?" Mary asked.

"I think I do," Dickon told her. "I can also talk to squirrels and foxes and ponies."

Dickon and Mary sat for hours, talking and laughing. As the moments passed, Mary felt very comfortable around

him. He told her about the birds and the animals on the moor and about the flowers and spring. For the first time in her life, Mary was looking forward to spring.

Mary studied Dickon's face carefully. Suddenly, she clasped her hands together tightly, took a deep breath, and stared into his big, blue eyes.

"Dickon, can you keep a secret?" she asked seriously. She knew she was taking a big chance, but she felt sure she could trust her new friend.

Dickon looked puzzled, but his smile was sincere. "I keep secrets all the time," he said. "Sure, I can keep a secret!"

"I've stolen a garden!" Mary blurted out at once.

Dickon looked at her strangely.

"It isn't mine," Mary explained, "but nobody wants it. Nobody cares for it, and nobody ever goes into it. Perhaps everything is dead in it already, I don't know."

Mary told Dickon everything.

"They're letting it die!" she cried. "And I want it to live! It's my garden!

I found it," she added. "The robin
helped me."

"Where is it?" Dickon asked at once.

"Come with me and I'll show you,"
she said. She led him around the path
along the wall to where the ivy grew thick.
When they came to the door, Dickon's eyes
were wide with excitement. Mary took out
her key, checked to make sure no one was
watching, and unlocked the door. Leading
Dickon inside, she quickly shut the door
behind them.

"This is it," she said proudly. "It's a

Secret Garden, and I'm the only one in the world who wants it to be alive!"

Dickon stood very still, gazing around the garden in wonder.

"It's just like a dream," he said breathlessly. "I never thought I'd see this place!"

"You mean you knew about it?" Mary asked.

Dickon nodded.

"Martha told me about it and how nobody ever went inside," he said. "I always wondered what it would be like!"

Mary pointed to the rose bushes. "Will there be roses?" she asked hopefully. "Are they all dead?"

"Not all of them," Dickon announced. "Look here." With a small knife, Dickon cut into a stem. "There's a lot of dead wood, but this part is wick. Right here where it's green.

"Wick?" Mary asked. "What's wick?"

"Alive," Dickon explained. "Don't worry, Mary. There will be many, many roses here this summer!"

Mary jumped joyfully. "I'm so glad it's wick!" she said happily. "I want them all to be wick. Let's go around the garden and count how many wick ones there are!"

They spent the rest of the afternoon running from place to place, examining the roses and trees. Dickon told Mary the garden needed a lot of work to get it in shape for summer.

"Will you come back and help?" Mary begged him. "I'll work in it every day, Dickon! I promise! Will you?"

"Sure!" Dickon answered. "It'll be great fun coming here and waking up the garden."

When it came time for dinner, Mary couldn't bear to leave. Dickon seemed too good to be true. She closed the door to the Secret Garden, then slowly faced him.

"Whatever happens," she asked, "you wouldn't tell?"

Dickon smiled and his cheeks grew redder than ever. "Never!" he assured her. "Your secret is safe with me."

Mary was sure that it was.

Chapter

9

Lord Craven

Mary ran back to the Manor so fast, she could barely catch her breath to tell Martha what had happened.

"Dickon!" she cried happily. "I've met Dickon!"

Mary told Martha all about the seeds and the gardening tools Dickon had brought. She told Martha all about their plans to start a big, beautiful garden.

"The only thing we need," she said, "is a bit of earth for our garden. Who should I ask?"

Martha thought for a minute. "Maybe Ben Weatherstaff," she suggested. "Your uncle lets him run the gardens as he likes, so maybe he's the one to ask. Your uncle likes him because he was a good friend to Lady Craven."

Mary was about to tell Martha more about her garden, when Mrs. Medlock appeared in the dining room. She looked as dreary as ever, but her eyes shot open in surprise when she saw Mary.

"My, you've... changed!" she exclaimed. Indeed, Mary was quite different from the day Mrs. Medlock had met her. "Something here agrees with you," she commented.

"It's the outdoors," Martha told her.

Mrs. Medlock looked at Martha, then back to Mary. "Go brush your hair," she ordered. "Martha, help Mary slip on her best dress. Mary's uncle has returned and he wishes to see her before he leaves again."

The color drained from Mary's face. Her heart began to thump and she felt herself turning back into her old, frail self. She said nothing while Martha helped her get dressed. Then, she followed Mrs. Medlock to the west wing in silence.

Mary was taken to a part of the house she had never been to before. At last, Mrs. Medlock knocked at a door.

"Come in," someone said from inside.

In the dark room, a man sat in a huge armchair by a glowing fire. His hair was black, but streaked with white. Mary peeked at his face and decided he could

have been handsome, had he not looked so miserable.

"Sir, this is Mary," Mrs. Medlock said.

"Leave her here," Lord Craven said. "I will ring for you when I want you to take her away."

Mary's legs trembled slightly when Mrs. Medlock left the room.

"Come closer!" he said finally.

Mary walked over to him and stood stiffly by his armchair.

"Are you well?" her uncle asked.

"Yes," she answered timidly.

"You look a little thin," he commented.

"But I am getting healthier," Mary answered. What an unhappy face he had!

"I'd forgotten all about you," her uncle said. "I'd intended to have a governess sent to you, but I have been so busy that I forgot."

"That's all right" Mary said quietly. "I don't need a governess."

"That is what Mrs. Sowerby said," her uncle muttered.

"Mrs. Sowerby?" Mary asked. "Is that Martha's mother?"

Lord Craven shifted in his chair and stared for a moment at his niece. "Yes," he said.

"She knows about children," Mary went on. "She has twelve herself."

Mary's uncle was still staring at her. "Well, what would you like to do?"

Mary hoped her voice would not tremble. "Play outdoors," she answered right away. "I never liked it in India. But here, the outdoors makes me feel good."

"Where do you play outdoors?" Lord Craven asked.

"Everywhere," Mary answered. "Martha bought me a skipping rope. I skip and run. I look around the gardens to see what is beginning to bloom. I'm not doing any harm," she added nervously.

"Don't look so frightened," Lord Craven said gently. "How could a child like you do any harm? You may do what you like."

Mary felt an excited lump in her throat.

"I am your guardian," Lord Craven went on, "though I am a poor guardian for any child. I cannot give you time or attention. I am too ill and distracted. But I wish you to be happy and comfortable. I don't know anything about children, but Mrs. Medlock will see that you have everything you need." He gazed at her more closely. "Do you need any toys? Or dolls? Or books?"

Mary took a deep breath and somehow got up the courage to ask. "Might I . . .?" she began timidly, "might I have a bit of earth?"

"Earth?" her uncle asked in confusion.

"To plant seeds in and watch things grow," Mary explained. "I'd like to start my own garden."

Lord Craven rubbed his chin thoughtfully. He had a far away look in his eyes, as if he was thinking about the past. "You like gardens, do you?"

Mary nodded.

"You can have as much earth as you want," he said.

Her uncle stood and began to walk slowly around the room. Mary noticed his back was hardly crooked at all. In fact, if you didn't know it was, you couldn't tell at all.

"You remind me of someone else who loved the earth and things that grow. When you see a bit of earth you want, take it. Make it come alive."

Mary was so excited she thought she might burst. But she kept calm until she was back in her room with Martha.

"I can have my garden!" she cried happily. "I may have it wherever I like! And I don't need a governess just yet!"

Martha smiled. "That was nice of him, eh?"

"Martha," Mary said gently, "he's really a nice man. Only, his face is so miserable and his forehead is all drawn together. It makes me unhappy to see him so miserable."

Martha nodded solemnly and went back to tidying up Mary's room.

Part

3

Chapter

A Cry in the Night

It rained hard that night, and Mary awakened to the sound of heavy raindrops beating against her window. The wind was whistling loudly through the Manor, so she could not get back to sleep.

Mary tossed and turned for nearly an hour, when something suddenly made her sit up in bed. It was a strange noise coming from down the hall.

"That isn't the wind," she told herself. "That is the sound of somebody crying!"

Mary got out of bed and went over to

her door. Poking her head into the hallway, Mary listened carefully for a few minutes. She was positive that she heard crying.

"I must find out who is crying!" she said.

Mary took the candle by her bedside and went quietly out of her room. The halls were long and dark, but she didn't

mind. She was determined to find out who was crying so horribly.

Walking down hallway after hallway, she turned left, then right, then left again. She came nearer to the crying. Clutching her candle, Mary kept walking. Her heart was beating so loudly, she was sure it would give her away!

The crying, Mary discovered, was coming from behind a large door. It was slightly open, so Mary pushed it gently, opening it further. She peeked into the room and gasped in shock. Mary thought for sure she was dreaming.

It was a big room, furnished with beautiful furniture. There was a small fire burning in the fireplace, and a candle flickering next to a huge bed. On the bed, a young boy cried fretfully.

Mary stood by the door, gaping at the boy. Her candlelight caught his attention, and he turned his head and stared back at her with very wide eyes.

"Who are you?" he whispered between sobs. "Are you a ghost?"

"No," Mary managed to reply. "Are you?"

The boy continued to stare and stare at Mary. He could not take his eyes off her.

"No," he said finally. "I am Colin."

"Colin?" Mary asked.

"Colin Craven," the boy answered. "Who are you?"

"I am Mary Lennox. Lord Craven is my uncle."

"He's my father," Colin said.

Mary gasped. "Your father? But no one told me he had a boy!"

Colin kept his eyes on her. He had stopped crying and was now studying Mary.

"Come here," he said.

Mary approached the bed, and Colin reached out his hand and touched her arm.

"You are real," he announced. "I have such real dreams sometimes. I thought you might be one of them. Where did you come from?"

"From my room," Mary told him. "The rain woke me up, and then I heard someone crying and wanted to find out who it was. Why were you crying?"

"Because I couldn't sleep. My head aches. What was your name again?" he asked, sitting up slightly.

"Mary Lennox. Didn't anyone tell you I had come to live here?"

Colin shook his head. "No. They wouldn't dare."

Mary was confused. "Why not?"

"Because they know I would only be afraid you might see me. I don't like it when people look at me."

"Why?" Mary asked.

"Because I am always very ill. I am always lying in this bed. My father won't

let people see me. The servants are not allowed to look at me or speak about me, either."

Mary pulled a chair next to Colin's bed and sat down. "This is certainly a strange house!" she said. "Everything is such a secret. Rooms are locked up and gardens are locked up—and you! Have you been locked up, too?"

"No," said Colin. "I stay in this room because it tires me to move out of it."

"Does your father come to see you?" Mary asked.

"Sometimes," Colin replied. "Usually he comes when I'm asleep. I don't think he wants to see me."

Mary looked at Colin. "Why?"

"My mother died when I was a baby, and it makes him sad to look at me," Colin explained. "He thinks I don't know, but I've heard people say that's the reason he can't bear to look at me."

Mary glanced around the room. "Have you always been here?" she asked.

"Yes," Colin replied quietly. "I used to

be taken out of the house, but people would always stare at me. Now I stay in all the time. My doctor, Doctor Craven, says I ought to get fresh air, but I hate fresh air."

"I didn't like it either when I first came," Mary told him. "But now I like it very much."

"I don't know anything about you. Tell me everything," Colin said.

Mary took a deep breath and told Colin about India, about her parents dying, and about how she came to Misselthwaite Manor. Colin had many questions, and Mary answered all of them.

From Colin, Mary learned that her uncle rarely visited his son, but he sent Colin books and toys. She also learned that Colin usually stayed in bed and ordered everyone around.

"Everyone must do what I ask," he told Mary. "I get sick when I'm angry, and no one wants me to be sick. My father has instructed everyone to do exactly what I want."

Mary thought Colin reminded her of a

Rajah prince she knew in India who had many servants and liked to order them around.

"How old are you?" Colin asked.

"Almost ten," she answered. "Like you."

Colin's large eyes peered suspiciously at Mary. "How do you know I'm ten?" he demanded.

"Because you said your mother died when you were born, and that's when the garden door was locked and the key was buried," Mary replied.

Colin leaned toward her. "What are you talking about? What garden?"

Mary hesitated for a second. She couldn't believe Colin didn't know about the garden that had been his mother's favorite place.

"The garden your father hates," she replied. "He locked it up after your mother died, and no one is allowed to go in it. No one even knows where the key is. He buried it."

Colin wanted to know all about the

garden. Mary told him all she knew, but she didn't want him to know she had found the garden. She didn't know Colin that well, and she wasn't sure she could trust him.

"Just how sick are you?" Mary asked slowly.

"Oh, I'm supposed to die," Colin replied flatly. "Ever since I can remember, I have heard people say that I'm going to die soon. At first they thought I was too little to understand, and now they think I can't hear them when they say it. But I can."

"Don't you want to live?" Mary asked.

"No," Colin said, "but I don't want to die either. I just don't like being sick all the time. I really don't want to talk about this. Let's talk about the garden. Don't you want to see it?"

Mary bit her bottom lip. "Yes," she replied gently.

"I do, too," Colin proclaimed. "I never wanted to see anything more in my life! I want to find that key and unlock the door.

I could go there in my wheelchair." Colin's expression changed suddenly. "I'm going to make them open that door!" he announced.

Mary gasped quietly. That would ruin everything! Everyone would know her secret!

"Oh, no! Don't do that!" Mary cried.

"But they have to listen to me," Colin protested. "I thought you wanted to see it!"

"I *do* want to see it," Mary said with a

lump in her throat. "But if you make them open the door," she said thinking quickly, "then it will never be a secret again."

"What do you mean?" Colin asked.

Mary pulled her chair closer to Colin. "You see," she said in a very low voice, "if no one knows about the garden but us, and there was a door hidden somewhere, and we found it, then we could go into the Secret Garden together and shut the door behind us. No one would ever know we were there! We could pretend that it was our garden. We could play there every day and plant seeds and make it blossom and come alive! Don't you see how much nicer it would be if it were kept a secret?"

Colin dropped back on his pillow. His pale face had just a hint of color, and Mary could tell he liked the idea.

"I never had a secret before," Colin said.

"This will be a great secret!" Mary announced. "I promise. Every day I'll go out and look for the key and the door. I'm so sure I'll find it! Then maybe we can find a boy to push you in your chair, and we could go alone to the Secret Garden!"

"I would really like that," Colin said, yawning slightly.

Colin lay still and listened as Mary talked about the garden and all the beautiful plants and flowers they could grow there. She talked about the birds and the baby animals who would live in their garden.

"When you find the garden," Colin said, rubbing his eyes, "then we can visit it every day. I'm glad you came here, Mary."

"So am I," Mary said. "I'll come as often as I can," she added, "but I will have to look for the garden every day."

Colin's eyes were closing. "Yes, you must," he said sleepily.

Mary sang softly to Colin, a song that her Ayah used to sing to her to help her sleep. A moment later, Colin was fast asleep.

Chapter

11

Martha Finds Out

By morning, the rain was coming down even harder than it had the night before. Mary knew there would be no going to the garden. She frowned and picked at her breakfast.

"What's with you this morning?" Martha asked her.

Mary peered up at her. "I found out who's been crying," she announced.

Martha gasped in horror. "No!"

"I heard it last night," Mary said. "And I got up to see where it was com-

ing from. It was Colin. I found him."

Martha's face turned red with fright. "Oh, Miss Mary! You shouldn't have! You'll get me in trouble! I'll lose my job!"

"You won't lose your job, Martha. Colin was glad that I came. We talked for a long time."

Martha looked at Mary in amazement. "He didn't scream and send you away?" she asked.

"No," Mary replied. "I asked if he wanted me to leave but he said no. He asked me questions about India and about gardens. He wouldn't let me go. Before I left, I sent him to sleep."

Martha looked as though she might faint from shock. "I can't believe it!" she cried. "He never lets strangers look at him!"

"Well, he let me look," Mary said, "and now he wants me to come see him every day. You must let me know when he wants me to come."

Martha began clearing away Mary's breakfast. Mary watched her walk nervously around the table. Martha's hands were shaking so, she nearly dropped her tray.

"Martha, what's the matter with Colin?" Mary asked curiously.

"No one knows for sure," Martha replied, taking a seat next to Mary. "When Lady Craven died, Colin was just an infant. Lord Craven was so upset that he refused to see the baby. He said the baby would just grow up with a crooked back like him!"

"But Colin doesn't have a crooked back," Mary pointed out.

"No, but everyone's been so afraid of his back becoming crooked, they've kept him in bed. He never gets up. He never goes out. He's grown so weak."

"He's still very spoiled," Mary said.

"Oh, he's worse now than he ever was!" Martha exclaimed. "He's been sick a couple of times, just from being kept in bed all the time. Because he is so weak, common colds nearly kill him!"

"Do you think he'll die?" Mary asked.

"If he never gets fresh air and does nothing but lie on his back in bed and take medicine, he just might!"

Mary stared at her plate. "Don't you think," she said thoughtfully, "that Colin would be much better outdoors in a garden, watching everything grow?"

Martha shook her head sadly. "One of the worst fits he ever had," she said,

"was when they took him out to the rose garden by the fountain. He had read in the newspaper about people getting sick from roses. When he sneezed, he began to shake and scream at everybody. He demanded to be brought back to the house. He cried himself into a fever and was angry and yelling at everyone."

"Well, if he ever yells at me," Mary said, folding her arms across her chest, "I won't ever visit him again!"

Martha was about to reply, when a bell rang in the kitchen. She jumped up from the table and ran out of the dining room. When she returned a few moments later, she had a puzzled look on her face.

"Master Colin wants to see you," she said to Mary. "Right away!"

Chapter

12

Visiting Her New Friend

In the daylight, Mary saw that Colin's room was indeed beautiful. There were colorful pictures and rugs hanging on the walls, and there was a big book-shelf lined with books. Colin was wrapped in a velvet dressing gown and sat up in bed against a large cushion. He was happy to see her.

"Mary!" he called out excitedly.

Mary smiled and nudged her head toward Martha, who was standing in the doorway, trembling. It was obvious that

Martha was very much afraid of losing her job.

Colin looked confused for a moment, then realized what was wrong with Martha.

"Martha," he ordered, "come here."

Martha was still shaking as she approached his bed.

"You are supposed to do whatever I please, right?" he asked.

"Yes, sir," Martha replied.

"And Medlock, she is to do what I please, too, right?"

"Yes, sir," Martha said.

"Well, if I order you to bring Miss Mary to me," Colin reasoned, "then how can you lose your job if Medlock finds out? You will only be doing exactly as I please. So you must not worry."

Martha turned to look at Mary, who was nodding in agreement with Colin. Martha seemed relieved.

"Thank you, sir," she said, bowing a short curtsy.

"If you obey me," Colin said grandly, "then I will take care of you. Now go away."

When the door closed behind Martha, Colin turned to see Mary eyeing him strangely.

"What?" Colin asked. "Why are you looking at me like that?"

"I was thinking two things," Mary said. "The first is how much you remind me of a Rajah prince I knew in India. He wore rubies and diamonds all over his clothes, and he spoke to everybody like you just spoke to Martha. Everybody had

to do everything he said—in a minute! I
think he had them killed if they didn't!"

Colin stared at her blankly. "And the
other thing?"

"I was thinking how different you are
from Dickon," she told him.

"Who is Dickon?" Colin demanded.

Mary's eyes lit up when she told
Colin about Dickon. She told how Dickon
knew everything and how he could charm
animals.

"He's not like anyone else in the
world!" Mary said. "He can charm foxes
and squirrels and birds, just like the

snake charmers in India. He plays tunes on a wooden pipe, and they come to listen! He knows all about gardens, and he knows about everything that grows on the moor."

"The moor is such a dreary place," Colin said, turning up his nose.

"I used to think that, too," Mary said at once. "But then Dickon told me about all the beautiful things that live and grow on the moor. When Dickon talks about it, you feel you must see it for yourself."

"I'll never see it," Colin muttered sadly.

"Not if you stay in this room forever," Mary said. Then she thought for a moment. "But maybe, you could see it someday."

Colin's eyes widened. "Go on the moor? How could I? I am going to die."

Mary placed her hands on her hips. "How do you know that?" she demanded. She hated the way Colin kept talking about dying.

"That's what everybody always says,"

Colin replied. "They all say it. Everyone except a doctor that I once had. He said, 'The lad might live if he made up his mind to do it. He needs a bit of cheering.' But they got rid of that doctor."

Mary suddenly became excited. "I know who could cheer you up!" she announced. "Dickon! He is always talking about live things. He never talks about dead things. He has such round, blue eyes and red cheeks, he's always cheery!"

Colin stared at her unsurely. "But . . ."

"Never mind!" Mary said, cutting him off. "Let's not talk anymore about dying. I don't like it. Let's only talk about living. And about Dickon."

Mary told as many stories about Dickon as she could. She remembered everything Martha had said. Soon, Colin was laughing as hard as Mary laughed, enjoying himself as he never had before. He didn't even realize it, but he was sitting up straight, without one single complaint about his back.

Mary kept Colin in a great mood, talking about Dickon, the red-breasted robin, and Ben Weatherstaff. They were both laughing so hard, they didn't hear the bedroom door open.

"Good Lord," a voice boomed into the room.

Colin and Mary stopped laughing and turned toward the door. It was Mrs. Medlock and Doctor Craven. Their eyes were wide with disbelief.

"What is going on?" Mrs. Medlock asked in a stunned voice.

Mary watched as Colin turned into a Rajah again.

"This is my cousin Mary Lennox," he announced coldly. "I asked her to come and talk to me. I like her. She must come whenever I send for her."

"But how . . ." started Mrs. Medlock, looking from Mary to Colin, then back to Mary.

"She heard me crying and found me herself," Colin explained.

"This is too much excitement for you," Doctor Craven said, rushing to Colin's bedside to take his pulse.

"Nonsense!" Colin replied, pulling his arm away. "She makes me better. She makes me forget that I am so ill."

Doctor Craven and Mrs. Medlock stood and stared for a moment longer. There was nothing more they could say. Colin had made up his mind. Mary was to be his new friend. Nobody could stop him from seeing her.

Chapter

13

Making New Plans

It rained for a whole week. Although she couldn't visit the Secret Garden or see Dickon, Mary enjoyed playing with Colin every day. Together, they read books, played games, and told stories. Except for the fact that he was always lying in bed, Colin looked happy.

Mrs. Medlock was shocked at the change in Colin. "I know I should be angry with you for going against my orders and snooping around," she scolded Mary one afternoon, "but I believe you have done that boy a world of good!"

One morning, Mary had an idea. "I know you don't like it when strangers look at you," she said to Colin, "but would it be all right if I asked Dickon to come meet you?"

Colin's eyes lit up. "Dickon is not a stranger!" he cried. "I know him so well from your stories, I feel as if I've already met him. I would very much like to meet Dickon."

Several days later, Mary awoke one morning to see the sun shining through her window.

"It's warm!" she cried, jumping out of bed. "The spring is here!"

It was early, but Mary was now able to dress herself. She got ready and ran outdoors, before even seeing Martha. She desperately wanted to visit her Secret Garden. When she got outside, she ran all the way there.

Mary found the ivy-covered door and pushed it open. She skipped inside, taking a deep breath of the fresh air.

"It smells nice, eh?" a voice said.

Mary jumped. "Dickon!" she cried out. "You startled me! How did you get here so early?"

Dickon laughed. "I've been up for hours," he told her. "As soon as the sun came up, I left my cottage. I just couldn't keep away from the garden any longer!"

It was just then that Mary noticed Dickon was not alone. Next to him, sitting under an apple tree, was a little red fox! And a crow perched on a branch over his head.

"This is the little fox cub I told you about," Dickon said. "His name is Captain. And this here's Soot. He came across the moor with me."

Mary smiled at the creatures, then something on the ground caught her eye.

"Dickon, look! Our flowers!" Mary knelt down and caressed the purple and orange and gold flowers that peeked out from the earth.

Mary and Dickon laughed and ran across the garden, marveling at how it was beginning to come alive. Mary felt so happy, she wished she could stay in the garden forever. That's when she remembered Colin.

"Dickon, there is something I want to tell you."

"Another secret?" Dickon asked with a grin.

Mary nodded. "Do you know about—Colin?" she asked slowly.

Dickon lifted his head and stared at her. "Do you?" he asked cautiously.

Mary nodded again. "I've seen him. I've been to see him every day this week.

He wants me to come. He says I'm making him forget about being sick and dying."

Dickon seemed surprised, and a little relieved. "Well, I'm glad you found him yourself. It was hard for me, knowing about him and not being able to say anything."

"How did you know about Colin?" Mary asked.

"Everybody knows about him, but nobody talks about him because he doesn't like it. Everyone feels sorry for Colin because he's crippled. Folks say he has his mother's eyes and because of that, his father can't bear to look at him."

"Well, all he talks about is dying," Mary said. "And I hate when he does it. He's very afraid of getting a crooked back like his father. He checks his back for lumps hundreds of times every day! He says that if he ever feels a lump, he might go crazy and scream himself to death!"

Dickon's eyes grew wide. "He shouldn't be thinking things like that.

Nobody could ever get well, lying around all day, thinking of things like that."

Mary nodded in agreement. "I was thinking," she said, "that if Colin came to our garden, then he wouldn't be waiting for lumps to grow on his back! If he was here, he'd be waiting for buds to break on those rose bushes instead! He'd most likely be healthier out here, too, in the fresh air."

Dickon liked the idea. "How can we get him to come out with us?" he asked.

Mary looked thoughtful. "I've been wondering that myself," she said. "I think about it all the time I talk to him. I wonder if he could keep it a secret. I wonder if we could bring him here without anyone seeing us. Maybe if you pushed his carriage," Mary suggested.

Dickon nodded.

"He could order all the gardeners to keep away," Mary went on, planning. "Then no one would find out."

Dickon petted Captain's back. "I hope he agrees, Mary. I bet that if he comes out here, he'll get well completely!"

Chapter

14

An Argument

Mary ate lunch quickly that afternoon. She was eager to get back to the garden.

"Master Colin wishes to see you," Martha told her, as Mary was on her way out the door.

"But I can't," Mary said. "Dickon is waiting for me. I'll see Colin later."

That afternoon, the garden was even lovelier. Mary and Dickon had managed to clear almost all the weeds out of the flower beds.

By the time Mary returned to the Manor, she was exhausted. Martha greeted her with a sad look and disturbing news.

"I wish you had gone to see Master Colin," Martha said, shaking her head. "He threw one of his fits when you didn't show up."

Mary went immediately to see Colin. He was lying in bed with the most sour expression. When he saw Mary, he turned the other way.

"Why didn't you come?" Colin asked without looking at her.

"I was working in the garden with Dickon," Mary replied.

Colin's face grew angry and red. "I won't let that boy come here anymore if you go see him instead of coming to see me!" he cried angrily.

Mary felt her face get hot. "If you send Dickon away," she warned. "I'll never come see you again!"

Colin faced her. "You'll have to if I want you to!" he yelled.

"I won't!" Mary yelled back.

"I'll make you!" Colin cried. "I'll have them drag you here!"

Mary folded her arms. "Oh, really, Master? Well, they may drag me here, but they can't make me talk when I get here! I'll sit and clench my teeth, and I won't tell you a thing! I won't even look at you. I'll sit and stare at the floor!"

"You are so selfish!" Colin screamed at her.

Mary looked shocked. "Me? What about you? You are the most selfish boy that ever lived!"

"I'm not selfish," Colin insisted. "I'm the one who is going to die. I have lumps

on my back, and they're growing bigger and bigger. I'm going to die!"

"You are not going to die!" Mary shot back.

Colin stared at her in disbelief. He was suddenly speechless. He had never heard anyone say he wasn't going to die before.

"I'm... I'm not?" he said in confusion. "But I am! Everyone says so!"

"Well, I don't believe it!" Mary protested. "You just say that so people will feel sorry for you."

Colin began to get hysterical. "I am dying! I am!" he shouted at Mary. "I want you to get out of my room! Now!"

Mary was surprised that Colin would throw her out of his room, but she was so upset with him, she was happy to go.

"Fine with me!" she yelled to him, slamming the door behind her. She could hear him cry out as she walked away. She had to hold her hands over her ears and run to her room.

Chapter

15

Forgiveness

In the middle of the night, Mary awoke to the sounds of horrible screaming.

She jumped out of bed and ran through the halls to Colin's room. Outside his door, Mrs. Medlock was speaking in hushed tones to Martha and Colin's nurse. Inside, the screaming grew louder.

"It's Colin," Mrs. Medlock told Mary. "He's having one of his fits."

"He can't calm down!" Martha cried. "No one can do anything! Mary, please, see

what you can do. He likes you. Please!"

"He threw me out of his room today," Mary told them.

"Please!" Martha cried again.

Mary was furious. Colin was scream-ing so hard, he'd probably forgotten why he was upset.

In a rage, Mary flung open his bed-room door.

"Stop it!" she yelled at him. "Stop it! You're driving everyone crazy!"

Colin sat up when he heard Mary's voice. His face was red and swollen from crying. He was sobbing so hard, he couldn't catch his breath.

"I... can't... stop," he gasped. "I... can't!"

"Yes you can!" Mary shouted. "Half of what is making you sick is your temper!" She stamped her foot.

"I felt a lump!" Colin choked. "Now I'll get a crooked back and die!"

"You didn't feel a lump," Mary insisted. "If you did, you imagined it! Turn over and let me see this lump.

Nurse!" she called out. "Will you come here and look at his back!"

The nurse turned Colin over and rolled up his shirt. Mary looked at Colin's thin, pale back.

"Not a single lump!" she announced.

The nurse rolled him back over. Colin gasped to catch his breath.

"No... no lump?" he asked.

Mary shook her head.

Colin gazed at Mary, his face streaked with tears. "You mean I'm going to live?"

"Probably," Mary answered flatly. "If you do away with that terrible temper."

Colin was worn out from all his carrying on. He lay against his pillow, sniffing back the tears.

"You need fresh air, too," Mary told him. "It will help you like it has helped me."

Colin was silent for a moment.

"I'll go out with you, Mary," he finally said. "I won't hate fresh air if we find... " He stopped himself because the nurse was still in the room. "That is, if I go out with you and Dickon. Dickon can push my chair. I really want to see Dickon and the fox and the robin."

Mary suddenly began to feel sad for her friend. It wasn't his fault he'd been stuck in his room for all these years. She pulled up his covers and sent the nurse out of the room.

"Would you like me to sing to you?" she asked gently.

Colin smiled a drowsy smile. "Oh, yes! It will help me sleep."

Mary sang softly as Colin quieted down. Soon, he fell asleep smiling.

Chapter

16

Colin and the Lamb

ꝏ

The next morning, Mary ran to meet Dickon in the garden. When she first saw him, she couldn't help but giggle. Dickon had a squirrel peeking out from each of his pockets.

Dickon grinned and introduced Mary to the squirrels. "This is Nut and this is Shell," he said. Mary giggled even harder when Nut and Shell leaped onto his shoulders at the sound of their names.

Dickon settled down under his favorite tree and took out his wooden pipe.

"Colin wants to meet you," Mary told him. "And Nut and Shell, too, of course!"

When Mary returned to the Manor for lunch, she visited Colin before going to eat. She sat next to his bed and told him about Dickon and Nut and Shell. Colin laughed so hard that tears came to his eyes. Mary could see he was feeling much better.

"Oh, I wish I could see them!" Colin cried, still laughing.

Mary raised her eyebrows. "Well, I'm glad you said that, Colin," she announced. "Because I have a big surprise for you!"

Colin straightened up in bed and looked Mary in the eye. "What?" he asked eagerly. "What?"

Mary was so anxious, she got up from her chair and sat next to him on his bed. "Can I trust you?" she asked in a whisper. "Can I trust you for sure?"

"Yes!" Colin whispered back. "Yes!"

"Dickon is coming to see you later today, and he's bringing his creatures with him!" she announced.

Colin cried out in delight.

"That's not all," Mary added. "The rest is better. There is a door into the garden. I found it! It was under the ivy on the wall. And I found a key, too. It was buried near the door!"

If Colin had been a strong, healthy boy, he probably would have jumped up and shouted with glee. But since he was weak, all he could manage was a soft "Hooray!"

"Oh, Mary!" he sighed. "Can I see the Secret Garden? Will I live to see it?"

Mary rolled her eyes. "Don't be silly,

Colin!" she said. "Of course you will!"

The way she said it so naturally brought Colin to his senses. Soon he was laughing at himself for being so silly.

Mary and Colin ate lunch together in Colin's room. When they finished, Doctor Craven came to examine Colin. "I thought you did not like fresh air," Doctor Craven said when Colin announced his plans to go outside with Mary.

"My cousin will take care of me," Colin told him. "She will go with me."

"And the nurse?" Doctor Craven asked.

Colin shook his head fiercely. "No. I don't want the nurse with me. Mary knows a boy who can push my carriage."

"It's Dickon," Mary chimed in.

Doctor Craven nodded. "If it is Dickon, then you will be okay. He's a strong, capable boy, that Dickon."

Downstairs, Mrs. Medlock walked Doctor Craven to the door.

"Can you believe it?" she asked.

"If I hadn't seen it with my own eyes,"

Doctor Craven said, shaking his head, "I never would have."

Back in Colin's room, Mary threw open the bedroom windows. "It's so beautiful!" she cried, taking in a deep breath. "The spring is the most beautiful thing I have ever seen! That's fresh air, Colin. Breathe it in!"

Colin lay in bed with his eyes closed, taking deep breaths. Mary had never seen him looking so relaxed.

Suddenly, Mary let out a small cry. Colin opened his eyes instantly.

"What is it?" he asked.

"Did you hear that caw?" Mary asked him.

Colin listened. Seconds later, there was another caw.

"Yes!" he replied. "I heard it!"

"That's Soot," Mary told him. "And listen more carefully. Do you hear a tiny bleat?"

"Oh, yes!" Colin cried.

"That's Dickon's newborn lamb. He found it on the moor yesterday all sick and dying. He nursed it back to health!"

Moments later, they heard Dickon and his animal friends coming down the corridor to Colin's room.

"If you please, sir," Martha said, opening Colin's door all the way, "here is Dickon and his creatures."

Dickon came in smiling his nicest, widest smile. He cradled the newborn lamb in his arms and the little red fox trotted by his side. As usual, Nut was on his left shoulder, and Shell on his right.

Colin sat up slowly and stared in amazement at the parade, just as he had stared at Mary when he saw her for the first time.

Dickon smiled at Colin, then walked up to him and put the lamb right on Colin's lap. The small creature immediately began to nuzzle his new caretaker.

"What's he doing?" Colin whispered.

"He's hungry," Dickon explained quietly, kneeling next to the lamb. Dickon took a bottle of milk from his pocket and offered it to the lamb. The lamb began to suck hungrily.

Everyone was quiet as the lamb ate. Pretty soon the tiny creature fell asleep on Colin's lap. In a voice barely above a whisper, Dickon told Colin the story of how he found the lamb and nursed him back to health.

As Dickon spoke, Soot flew around the room, sometimes flying out the open window, then back in again. Nut and Shell rested on the windowsill. Captain was curled up on the floor next to Dickon.

The three friends visited for nearly two hours. They looked at picture books of gardens and flowers, talking excitedly about their own garden.

Colin and Mary exchanged quiet looks. They were overjoyed. That was obvious.

Part

4

Chapter

17

Colin in the Garden

Unfortunately, Mary and Dickon had to wait a week before they could take Colin to the Secret Garden. The weather turned cold, too cold to go outdoors. Mary and Colin had to be content with talking about the garden and planning Colin's first trip to see it.

Finally, the day arrived. The sun was out, brighter than ever, and a gentle breeze blew. A footman named John was called to carry Colin down the stairs to where Mary and Dickon were waiting with Colin's chair.

Once Colin was settled in his chair, he made an announcement to Mrs. Medlock.

"I am going out into the gardens with Mary and Dickon today," he stated. "If the fresh air agrees with me, I may go out every day. When I'm out, none of the other servants or gardeners should be anywhere around. Everyone must keep away until I send word that they may go back to their work."

"Very well," she told him.

Outside the Manor, Dickon pushed the chair slowly and steadily along the path. Mary walked beside the chair and pointed out everything along the way. Colin leaned comfortably against a cushion and let the sun warm his face.

"The fresh air is wonderful!" he said, taking in a deep breath.

Finally, they came to the long, ivy-covered wall.

"This is it," Mary told Colin. "On the other side of this wall is the Secret Garden!"

Colin could barely contain his excitement. "The door! Let's go to the door!"

Mary pointed out all the things she'd told Colin about—the tree where she'd first seen the robin; Ben Weatherstaff's garden; the place where she had found the key; and, finally, the thick brush of ivy that covered the door.

"Here it is!" she sang excitedly, pushing the ivy away and revealing the thick wooden door.

Colin clasped his hands together excitedly.

Mary opened the door, and Dickon pushed the chair in quickly. Once inside, they both looked down at Colin, who covered his eyes with his hands. When they told him he was inside the garden, he uncovered his eyes slowly.

"Oh!" Colin gasped in delight. He looked around and around, not knowing what to say first. It was indeed a beautiful sight—the green leaves and the enormous trees, the purple and gold flowers, the

birds flying in the sky, and the sweet scent of roses.

Colin took it all in, then gazed up at Mary and Dickon. His smile was wider than ever and his dark eyes twinkled in the sunlight. "I will get better!" he announced to them. "I will get better and I will live forever and ever and ever!"

Dickon pushed Colin's chair into the shade, under the apple tree. From there, Colin could watch as Mary and Dickon weeded and planted. From time to time, they brought him things to look at—flower buds, twigs, a feather from a woodpecker. Every moment of the afternoon was full of new things to see.

When the sun was at its highest, Dickon took out his pipe and played sweet music. Colin was sure he had never been happier.

All at once, Mary heard a rustling of branches and looked up to the trees. "Colin!" she cried. "The robin!"

Colin looked up and saw the red-breasted robin Mary had told him about.

He leaned back on his cushion and watched the robin sing and fly about.

"He's beautiful!" Colin sighed.

Watching the robin, Colin soon fell asleep.

"Colin looks much better," Mary whispered to Dickon. "He has a rosy color in his face, and he looks almost normal."

"Our garden is good for him," Dickon agreed.

Mary and Dickon went back to their weeding and digging as Colin slept. When he awoke, they enjoyed a small picnic of hot tea and crumpets. Everyone broke into fits of laughter when Nut and Shell stole a few crumbs for themselves and scurried up a tree to feast.

"I don't want this afternoon to end," Colin said to his friends. "But I shall come back here with you every day."

"You'll get plenty of fresh air," Mary noted. "You'll get bigger and healthier in no time. Just like me!"

"And we'll have you walking about and digging right here with us," Dickon added.

Colin flushed a bright red and looked at Dickon with hopeful, wide eyes.

"Walk?" he gulped. "And dig? Do you really think I'll be able to?"

"Well sure!" Dickon replied. "You've got legs like the rest of us, haven't you?"

Mary glanced nervously at Dickon. They had never really asked Colin if there was anything the matter with his legs.

"Yes," Colin replied sullenly. "But they are so thin. They shake so much that I'm afraid to stand on them."

"Well," Dickon said, "when you stop being afraid, then you'll stand on them!"

Colin looked doubtful at first. Then he broke into a huge smile. "Yes!" was all he could manage to say.

Mary and Dickon went back to planting seeds and tending to the flower bed. Suddenly, Colin gasped with alarm.

"Who is that man?" he asked in a scared whisper.

"Man?" Mary and Dickon cried in unison. They followed Colin's gaze over to the high wall. It was Ben Weatherstaff, standing on a ladder on the other side of the wall. He was glaring at them as if he were very angry.

Chapter

18

Standing and Digging

"What are you doing here?" Ben Weatherstaff shouted at Mary. "You shouldn't have gone poking your nose back here. This garden is off limits! Lord Craven has ordered . . ."

He stopped suddenly when he saw Colin.

"Good Lord," he said, his voice barely above a whisper. Ben looked as if he'd seen a ghost.

"Wheel me over there!" Colin demanded from his chair.

Dickon pushed the carriage over to the wall.

"Do you know who I am?" Colin bellowed at the gardener.

Ben Weatherstaff couldn't answer. He just stared and stared at Colin. Then he rubbed his eyes and stared again. In a shaky voice he answered.

"It could only be you, Master Craven. I would know those eyes anywhere. They were the eyes of your mother! But I thought you were too crippled to be moved from the Manor."

Colin sat as straight and tall as possible.

"I am not a cripple!" he cried out furiously.

"He's not," Mary agreed. "I looked for a lump on his back. He doesn't have any!"

Ben Weatherstaff wiped his brow nervously. "You don't have a crooked back?" he asked.

"No!" Colin shouted.

"And you don't have crooked legs?"

The humiliation was more than Colin

could bear. Mary watched as her friend's face turned red. She knew that being accused of having crooked legs was bound to make Colin wild with anger. She silently prayed that he wouldn't have another fit.

Instead of screaming at Ben Weatherstaff, Colin surprised them all by pulling the blankets off his legs.

"Dickon!" he called out. "Come here!"

Dickon ran to his friend. Mary watched as Colin grabbed Dickon's arm and hoisted himself out of the chair. She held her breath when Colin's feet touched the ground. Then she smiled from ear to ear. Colin was standing upright!

"Look at me!" Colin cried to Ben Weatherstaff. "Just look at me!"

"He's as straight as I am!" Dickon called out. "He's as straight as any boy!"

Mary looked up at Ben Weatherstaff and was surprised to see he was crying.

"You're a fine lad!" the gardener cried. "God bless you!"

Colin held Dickon's arm tightly, but he didn't stumble or fall. He stood

straighter and straighter with each pass-
ing moment and looked Ben Weatherstaff
in the face.

"I'm your master when my father is
away," he said. "And you are to obey me.
This is my garden. You cannot tell anybody about it. Get down from your ladder

and come into the garden. You will have to be let in on our secret."

When Ben Weatherstaff was out of sight, Colin turned to his friends. "I can stand," he said proudly.

"I knew you could!" Dickon cheered.

"You just had to stop being afraid," Mary added.

Colin beamed at his friends and drew himself up even straighter.

"I'm going to walk to that tree," he announced, pointing to a tree a few feet away. "I want to be standing there when Ben Weatherstaff comes."

Colin walked to the tree and, though Dickon held his arm, he stood strong. He held himself straight so he looked tall.

"Look at me!" Colin called to Ben Weatherstaff. "Do you see a boy with a crooked back? Do you see a boy with crooked legs?"

"No, sir!" Ben Weatherstaff replied.

Colin cleared his throat. "This is my garden now," he said. "I will come here every day. But it is to be kept a secret.

My orders are that no one is to know that we come here. Dickon and my cousin have worked hard to make this garden come alive. I don't want to spoil it for them."

Ben Weatherstaff nodded and looked around. "Your mother loved this garden so," he said quietly. "She once told me,

'Ben, if I'm ever ill or go away, you must take care of my roses!' And I did! Every year I came over the wall and did a bit of pruning. But ever since my arthritis, I haven't been able to."

"That's why it was so wick!" Dickon remarked.

"I'm glad you kept your promise to my mother," Colin told him. "You know how to keep a secret."

Colin slowly dropped to his knees, but when Dickon ran over to help him, Colin waved him away.

"I want to dig, too!" he announced, grabbing a trowel from the dirt. Slowly, he began to scratch at the earth with the trowel. "Look! I'm digging! Standing, walking and digging all in one day!"

The sun began to set in the Secret Garden. The last thing Colin did on that first day of his new life was plant a rose for his mother. When the sun finally dropped below the wall of the garden, Colin again stood on his own two feet.

Chapter

19

Another Secret

The seeds Dickon and Mary planted blossomed, giving the garden the color and life it had missed for so many years. The rose bushes bloomed, too, climbing the trunks and walls like ivy. Day by day and hour by hour leaves grew and buds opened, filling the air with a sweet scent.

On the days that it didn't rain, the children worked and played in their garden. Colin was able to see it all. Every morning Dickon wheeled him out. For Colin it was wonderful enough just to lie on the grass and watch things grow.

Most fun of all was watching the creatures play in their garden. Nut and Shell and Captain and the robin amused them for hours. Each day, Dickon charmed a new creature on his way across the moor, bringing it to live in the Secret Garden. Soon there were rabbits and squirrels and foxes.

Each day, Colin grew stronger and stronger and walked a bit further. He was on his way to becoming completely well again.

Colin's speedy recovery presented a problem. The more Mrs. Medlock and Doctor Craven saw Colin get better, the more they spoke of writing to Colin's father to tell him the news. Colin wanted to be the one to tell the good news to his father. He longed to show his father that he was as normal as other boys.

So the children came up with a plan. In the garden, when they were alone, Colin was to walk and run and exercise as much as possible. But in front of Mrs.

Medlock and Doctor Craven, Colin would stay in his wheelchair and complain of aches and pains.

The only other person they all agreed to let in on their secret was Susan Sowerby, Dickon's mother. So one night, Dickon told his mother the whole story about the key and the door, and about how Mary found Colin. He also told her how Colin was walking and running like a normal boy.

Susan Sowerby was so happy to hear about Colin, she cried tears of joy.

"My word!" she exclaimed. "What a good thing it was when Mary came to live at Misselthwaite Manor! But what about Mrs. Medlock and the boy's doctor? What do they make of all this?"

"They don't know what to make of it!" Dickon told her. "Every day, Colin looks different. His face is all filled out, and that pale yellow color is completely gone! But he still has to do a bit of complaining," Dickon added with a sneaky grin.

Susan Sowerby stared at her son's twinkling eyes in confusion. "What do you mean?" she asked.

"He does it to keep them from guessing what's happened," Dickon explained. "If the doctor knew he could stand on his feet, he would write and tell Lord Craven. But Master Colin is saving that news. He wants to tell his father the secret himself. He's going to get bigger and stronger every day so that when his father returns he can show him he's healthy."

Dickon's mother chuckled.

"Master Colin is carried down to his

chair every day," Dickon went on happily. "And he yells at the footman, John, for not carrying him carefully! He tries to look as helpless as possible, so he groans and grunts when he is put in his chair. Then Mary says, 'Oh, poor Colin! Does it hurt much? Poor Colin!' They can hardly keep from laughing! When they're safely in the garden, Colin jumps up from his chair, and they laugh until they are completely out of breath!"

Susan Sowerby laughed, too. "I'm so glad to hear the boy is well," she exclaimed. Back at the Manor, Doctor Craven just shook his head. He had just finished examining Colin, who had been complaining of aches and pains all night. During the examination, Mary stood behind the doctor, making silly faces at Colin.

"I'll leave a bottle of pills with the nurse," Doctor Craven told Colin. "When your head and back aches again, she'll give you a pill."

"All right," Colin answered as weakly as possible. He tried desperately not to burst out laughing. When Doctor Craven left the room, he and Mary could hold it in no longer. They had to grab pillows from Colin's bed to muffle their laughter.

Chapter

20

Mrs. Sowerby Helps Out

By mid-summer the garden was in full bloom. Mary, Dickon, and Colin spent every single day there. One hot morning, Colin was working on a new flower bed when he dropped his trowel. He gazed down at his arms and legs and stood slowly, standing as tall as he could. All at once, he realized something.

"Mary! Dickon!" he cried. "Just look at me!"

They stopped their weeding and looked at him.

"Do you remember that first morning when you brought me here?" Colin asked.

Mary and Dickon both nodded.

"Just this minute," Colin said breathlessly, "I realized it. I looked at my hand digging with the trowel and I had to stand up to make sure it was all real. And it is real! I'm *well!* I'm *well!*"

"Oh, yes, Master Colin. You most certainly are!"

The children spun around to see who had spoken.

There stood Susan Sowerby with tears in her eyes, gazing admiringly at Colin.

"Mother!" Dickon cried happily.

Mary and Colin rushed to her, delighted to finally meet Dickon and Martha's mother.

"Even when I was sick," Colin told her, "I wanted to meet you."

Susan Sowerby still had tears in her eyes.

"Oh, my dear boy!" she said. "You look so much like your mother, it made

my heart jump. Just wait until your father sees you!"

Colin looked anxious. "Do you think he'll like me?" he asked hesitantly.

Susan Sowerby smiled. "Aye, for sure," she replied, giving him a hug. "And look at you!" she cried to Mary. "You look as healthy as my Elizabeth Ellen! I suppose you look like your mother, too. Martha tells me she was a beautiful woman. And you are just as pretty!"

Mary smiled shyly. Remembering how beautiful her mother was, she was glad to hear that she looked like her.

They showed Dickon's mother around their garden, then ate the wonderful lunch she had brought for them. Then, they played and sang for hours, until it was time to go home.

Susan Sowerby placed a hand on Colin's shoulder. "He will be home soon, I'm sure," she said gently. "And it will be so nice that you are the one to tell him. "You've certainly worked very hard in making sure of it, anyway!"

Colin laughed. "Every day I think about how I'm going to tell him. I think now that I just want to run into his room."

Susan Sowerby laughed out loud. "Oh, what I would give to see the look on his face!"

Miles away, in a beautiful Austrian village, Lord Archibald Craven walked slowly along the bank of a river. He stopped at one point and stared deep into the water, gazing at his reflection. But he

turned away quickly. His sad image was more than he could bear.

Lord Craven had been away from Misselthwaite Manor for a long, long time. He thought about his sick son back home. Tears came to his eyes. He felt sad and ashamed at having been such a horrible father. He hadn't meant to be. After his wife passed away, he couldn't bring himself to care for the boy. Then, as the years passed, Lord Craven had become more and more miserable and unhappy.

One night in the middle of the summer, Lord Craven had a dream. He dreamed that his wife was calling to him.

"Archie!" the sweet voice sang out. "Archie!"

In his dream, he answered her, "Lilias!" he cried. "Where are you?"

"In the garden!" she replied joyfully. "In the garden!" When Lord Craven woke, he felt strange. He had a sudden urge to see the garden his wife had loved so much. He wanted to see the garden he had locked up on the day she died.

Even stranger than the dream was
a letter he received at the Inn that very
afternoon. He opened it and read:

Dear Sir,

*I am Susan Sowerby. You came to
me many months ago for some advice
about your niece, Mary. Please, sir, I
would come home if I were you. I think
you would be glad to come home, and—if
you will excuse me, sir—I think your wife
would ask you to come if she were here.*

Respectfully,
Susan Sowerby

Lord Craven read the strange letter
twice before putting it back in its enve-
lope. He kept thinking about the dream.

"I must go back to Misselthwaite," he
said to himself. "I will go at once."

Chapter

21

Father, It's Me

A few days later, Lord Craven was in Yorkshire again, traveling home by railroad. During the entire trip he thought of nothing but his son. He thought of the poor boy lying in his dreary room in that sad bed.

Lord Craven cried, ashamed of how poorly he had treated Colin. He decided to visit Colin that night and beg for his forgiveness. Perhaps it was not too late to become a real father to his boy.

When Lord Craven arrived at the

Manor, it was midday and the sun was shining. He stood at the door to the Manor and looked out at his gardens. Everything looked beautiful, and he could smell the roses.

The roses immediately reminded him of his wife and the dream. How real that dream had been, he thought. How wonderful and clear the voice was when it called to him, "In the garden! In the garden!"

"I will try to find the key," he said. "I will try to open the door. I must."

Mrs. Medlock came up behind him. "Lord Craven! Welcome home!"

"Thank you," Lord Craven said. "How is Colin?" he inquired.

Mrs. Medlock had a strange look on her face. "He's . . . different," was all she could say.

"Where is Colin now?" Lord Craven asked.

"In the garden, sir. He's always in the garden. No one is allowed to go near. He doesn't want them looking at him."

Lord Craven barely heard her last words.

"In the garden," he repeated. *In the garden!*

Lord Craven walked along the path.

He passed Ben Weatherstaff's vegetable garden and went through the orchard. Soon he reached the high, ivy-covered wall. The sight of it made him tremble. It had been a long time since he had seen that wall.

He walked along the wall, trying to remember where he had buried the key. He walked slowly, searching every inch of the ground, but he just couldn't remember where he had buried it. Then, in a stroke of luck, Lord Craven found the door! And, to his surprise, it was *open!*

He stood very still, then reached out and pushed the door open further. Hearing a strange sound, he paused. No human being had passed through that door in ten years, but from inside the garden he was hearing sounds! Sounds of scuffling feet and muffled laughter. The laughter of . . . children.

Lord Craven was sure he was dreaming. But when he stepped into the garden, a boy suddenly burst forth at full speed and fell into Lord Craven's arms.

Dazed, Lord Craven caught the youngster. He held him away to get a better look. Suddenly he gasped with shock, seeing Colin's eyes, so big and gray.

"Father, it's me. Colin."

Lord Craven could not stop looking at Colin's face. He couldn't believe what he was seeing. "But, how . . ." he started to say.

"It was the garden," Colin told him. "And Mary and Dickon and the creatures. I wanted to keep it a secret until you came. I'm *well*, father!"

Lord Craven choked back the tears. Trembling with joy, he hugged his son tightly. "My son," he sobbed.

"Now it doesn't have to be a secret anymore," Colin said. "It will probably scare everyone out of their wits when they see me. I am never getting into that chair again. I shall walk back to the Manor with you, Father."

Ben Weatherstaff was bringing barrels of vegetables into Mrs. Medlock's kitchen, when he heard Martha's screams. Along with Mrs. Medlock and Doctor Craven, he ran down to the front door of the Manor.

"What is it, Martha?" Mrs. Medlock asked anxiously.

Martha was speechless. All she could do was point out the window to the two

figures walking up the path toward the Manor.

Mrs. Medlock followed her gaze. Suddenly, she screamed loud enough to attract every servant in the house.

Everyone watched as Lord Craven walked happily to the Manor. By his side, with his head held high in the air and his eyes full of laughter, was Master Colin Craven. The young boy was walking as strongly as any other ten-year-old boy!

The End

ABOUT THE AUTHOR

Frances Hodgson Burnett was born in 1849 in England. When Frances' father died three years later, her mother took over the family business. By the time Frances was in her teens, the business had begun to fail. The family crossed the Atlantic and settled in Knoxville, Tennessee.

Frances started writing as a way of helping support her family during those trying times. During her career, she wrote more than 40 books. Some of her works include *Little Lord Fauntleroy*, *A Little Princess*, and *The Secret Garden*.

Treasury of Illustrated Classics™

Adventures of Huckleberry Finn
The Adventures of Pinocchio
The Adventures of Robin Hood
The Adventures of Sherlock Holmes
The Adventures of Tom Sawyer
Alice in Wonderland
Anne of Green Gables
Beauty and the Beast
Black Beauty
The Call of the Wild
Frankenstein
Great Expectations
Gulliver's Travels
Heidi
Jane Eyre
Journey to the Center of the Earth
The Jungle Book
King Arthur and the Knights of the Round Table
The Legend of Sleepy Hollow & Rip Van Winkle
A Little Princess
Little Women
Moby Dick
Oliver Twist
Peter Pan
The Prince and the Pauper
Pygmalion
Rebecca of Sunnybrook Farm
Robinson Crusoe
The Secret Garden
Swiss Family Robinson
The Time Machine
Treasure Island
20,000 Leagues Under the Sea
White Fang
The Wind in the Willows
The Wizard of Oz